# OBITS FOR FUN

## ILLUSTRATED LIFE REVIEWS FOR THOSE DEPARTED

## LINDA A. LAVID

PLUM BARN PRESS
WESTFIELD, NY

Plum Barn Press
KDP Independent Imprint
Westfield, NY 14787


ISBN-13: 9781795719377

## Those Departed

| | |
|---|---|
| Lord Smith | Emma Vanderbilt |
| Essie Perry | Jimmie Valenti |
| Myra Pinkel | Pandora |
| Molly Mackay | Mercedes Camacho |
| Rosco Pillow | Mae Lou Higgins |
| Millie Bunford | Manford Peabody |
| KiKi Palmer | Tulip Maison |
| Richard Bean | Rupert Manning |
| Ruby Slippers | Henrik Johansen |
| Jasmine Dupont | Randall Lovitz |
| Artie Csonka | Herman Johnson |
| Maybelline Hatch | Namke Lewis |
| Thomas Wendell | Lance Woodsman |
| Lillian Farnsworth | Adelia Rosen |
| Harry Leonard | Creeley Messenger |
| Violet Ramsey | Sweet Pea Garrity |
| Eleanor Snow | Charles Longfellow |
| E.L. Stand | Dolly Warner |

Lord Smith checked out on Thursday. He is survived by two sons, Prince and Duke, whose whereabouts at this time are unknown. In the event that either one shows up at the executor's office (family lawyer), their collections of comic books are in the attic. Lord had a forty-year career at the post office which he despised. His obsession, for those fortunate to really know him, were his orchids. His book, *Orchids: My Perennial Bliss*, will be posthumously published.

Essie Perry died unexpectedly in her Lower West Side home surrounded (too closely) by her boa constrictor, Rushmore. Essie's penchant for snakes was renown. She often said, "Some men love me. Some men love my snakes. I'm looking for a man who loves us both." Rushmore was immediately removed from the premises. After some deliberation by city officials, the Humane Society, and Ms. Perry's executor, Rushmore was reunited with Essie. They will travel together in the afterlife.

Myra Pinkel passed over on Tuesday while in the supermarket checkout line. Ms. Pinkel was observed repositioning her shopping cart from different aisles seemingly trying to find a quicker line. When she finally settled into a spot, the cashier's register froze. In frustration, Ms. Pinkel grabbed some M&Ms, ripped open the package, and chugged the entire contents. Most went down the wrong pipe.

Molly Mackay was welcomed into spirit on Sunday. Miss Mackay, ordained as a Sister of St. Joseph, spent thirty years teaching six grade after which time, she retired from "the whole stinking morass" of Vatican rule, became a lay person, and fought tirelessly for the establishment of a women's ministry in the Catholic church. She is seen here with her Glock, retooled to shoot wax bullets that disintegrated upon discharge. "Sometimes it's the only way to get people's attention."

7

Rosco Pillow, ventriloquist for Smooth Eddy, died peacefully at home surrounded by family. Mr. Pillow played burlesque theaters throughout the US with his beloved puppet, Eddy, who would interact with the female audience using such memorable pick-up lines as: "Hey Baby, I'd like to use your thighs as earmuffs" and "Smile. It is the second best thing you can do with your lips.

Millie Bunford passed over on Tuesday. Millie, always unassuming and polite, gambled every morning from 7 to 9 in various Vegas casinos for the past thirty years. It was estimated Ms. Bunford made a small fortune on the house but was never banned since she attracted heavy-hitters far and wide. Ms. Bunford quipped with everyone, was a great tipper, and enjoyed her morning coffee with two shots of Baileys.

KiKi Palmer passed over to greener pastures where buffalo roam and deer and antelope play. Ironic since she hated the outdoors. KiKi is survived by her brother, Arthur, who came to her home every Sunday for the past forty years to enjoy a Manhattan. They usually ordered a pizza. Neither brother nor sister had married. According to KiKi, marriage was archaic. Two bulldogs, Daisy and Cornelius, are available for adoption at the K-9 Rescue.

10

Richard Bean, counter-culture poet, died yesterday. In 1972, Mr. Bean made headline news after he was denied tenure at the University of Buffalo, set up a tent on the grounds, and went on a hunger strike for two weeks. It was later revealed, a number of coeds were dropping off food and hallucinogens late at night. It was the two best weeks of his life. In his later years, Mr. Bean became a photographer. He is credited with the phrase "Oh, hell no."

Ruby Slippers (nee Nia Goldman) passed into spirit when Mars was in retrograde. Ruby, known for her support of the arts, started out in humble beginnings as a caged Go-Go dancer. From performance artist to professional party "It" girl, friends say her wit, charm, and remarkable networking skills, could have elected her President. In a recent interview, Ms. Slippers commented, "My only talent is remembering people's names."

Jasmine Jablonski Dupont, fashion icon, died as she had lived, in dramatic style. It was reported Mrs. Dupont tripped on a hand-painted silk caftan and fell down a marble staircase. On the day of her passing, Mrs. Dupont was quoted as saying, "American women are oinkers. British woman should be kenneled. And the French...don't get me started." Mrs. Dupont's response from the certain backlash will be missed. *Adieu ma douce.*

Artie Csonka, who passed on Thanksgiving, had emigrated from Hungary in the 1950s. Upon arriving in New York City, he immediately ordered a Coca Cola. Much to his shock, it was the foulest drink he had ever tasted. After that disappointment, he became a traveling performance artist, The Hat Man, specializing in chapeaugraphy (manipulation of felt hats). He often portrayed immigrant characters. His most beloved, Ziggy Datz, "from somevhere over dere."

Maybelline Hatch passed into the light on Tuesday. Maybelline fought tirelessly for the humane treatment of laboratory mice that are overfed and inactive which in turn makes them prone to cancer, type-2 diabetes, renal failure, and poor subjects for drug testing. Ms. Hatch often testified before the Subcommittee on Health wearing her trademark Minnie Mouse ears.

Thomas (TW) Wendell, the eccentric billionaire, was unable to be stabilized prior to being be cryonically suspended. According to the Life Extension Center, Mr. Wendell continued to take baby aspirin against advisement and subsequently bled internally. TW made his fortune with derivatives, the true weapons of mass destruction. Services will be held at an undisclosed abbey in Switzerland.

Lillian Farnsworth, proud centenarian, passed into the open arms of the Lord on Tuesday. Lillian, dearly loved by the staff of the Good Shepard Adult Home, was their media mascot for ten years. When asked the secret to a long life, she said, "How the eff would I know?" Her interviews were often edited. At the time of passing, she was eating Cheetos in the game room when B6 was called out. Her last word was "Bingo!"

Harry Leonard, Madison Avenue ad exec turned mass movement spinner, bought the farm on Tuesday. Mr. Leonard's career took a dramatic turn after he was struck by lightning on a golf course. Subsequent to the event, he sold all his belongings, dismantled a life of luxury, and became a spinner of slogans for grassroots movements in need of media attention. As part of the "We are the 99%" demand for a national work slowdown, Mr. Leonard coined the phrase, "Fridays are Optional".

Violet Ramsey died in her sleep surrounded by her remarkable collection of Barbie dolls. Miss Ramsey's career began as a Santa's helper on the 1960s hit, *Queen for a Day*. When the show was canceled, Violet went on to teach women how to showcase items advertised on television. Her credits included *Let's Make a Deal* and *The Price is Right.* "It's all about standing straight, smiling, and caressing the product with hand flourishes."

Artist, Eleanor Snow, passed over on Tuesday. Ms. Snow, a subversive artist of fifty years, used unconventional means to protest the unconscionable action of public and private institutions. Never using a brush, Ms. Snow splattered paint onto the exterior of buildings, where it would then drip. Her technique, known as the Ellie Drip, became common in abstract paintings. In recent years, she utilized paint bombs, calling her work, "ka-powing". While often arrested, she never served time, citing the First Amendment as her defense.

E. L. Stand, secluded visionary, non-conformist, and peace activist, passed to another dimension on Thursday. E. L., shown in this picture circa 1968, was part of the art and Studio 54 scene in the mid 70s. Often on the arm of the icons of the day: Andy Warhol, Elizabeth Taylor, E. L.'s sexual identity and orientation was never made public. E. L. was famous for saying, "I don't fall in love with a man or a woman, I fall in love with a person."

Emma Vanderbilt, commonly known as Miss Priss, the author of many books on etiquette, passed over on Tuesday. The go-to gal for decorum, Emma decried many heathen practices commonly in vogue. Wearing shorts to church, using paper towels for napkins, drinking red wine with fish, were a few of her rants. She will be buried, per her request, in a classic navy wool crepe suit with her signature white gloves and proper underwear.

Jimmie Valenti, seen here circa 1965, was one of the Four Lovers that in subsequent years became the Four Seasons. Jimmie's falsetto, revered in early songs, was soon exposed as a false falsetto due to the use of helium. After Jimmie left the group, Frankie Valli, having developed a natural technique, took over Jimmie's vacated spot. Mr. Valenti continued his singing career composing original music. His most famous song: "Jenny, Jenny Worth Every Penny"

Pandora died as she had lived with great elan and friends close by. Once a model, Pandora, in her later years, repurposed clothes from second-hand stores and showed regularly at Fashion Week. Tickets to her show became the most sought after. "Style," she had said, "is never static but builds on the foundations of movements, discoveries, art. It is a living history. To dress any other way is ignorant and a damn waste of money."

Mercedes Camacho, a native of Cuba, died in Havana surrounded by her extended loving family. At age 14, Ms. Camacho moved to New York City to be a star on Broadway. A long career followed as an understudy, walk-on, and stand-in for Rita Moreno, Chita Rivera, and the Chiquita Banana (Macy's Day Parade). An inveterate performer, Merche brightened every marginal role she played with infectious enthusiasm. She loved cigars, noting often, "With cigars, size doesn't matter. They're all good."

Mae Lou Higgins passed on after a short illness. Mae Lou was the town clerk for over forty years where she only missed one day. It was in 1983 when Ms. Higgins, not wanting to come to the office to conduct personal matters and renew her dog license, arrived at the town hall before business hours. After being turned away for not having the dog's shot records, Mae left the building and found her car ticketed for an expired parking meter. She then found the officer a couple of cars down, spit at him, and was taken into custody.

Manford Peabody, the entrepreneur who started tchotchke or souvenir shops, first in Coney Island, then later in tourist centers throughout the US, died in Shanghai where he had been on a business trip negotiating the bulk purchase of tiny plastic barrels, inscribed *Barrel to your Peril,* for his shop in Niagara Falls. In 2008, Mr. Peabody had made headline news stating his products were neither toys nor toxic. "They are memorabilia. Get over it."

Tulip Maison, diarist, died two days ago in France. A child prodigy, Ms. Maison, began writing at age six. Over the years, her memoirs were endlessly edited under the three voluminous titles: *Beginning. Middle. End.* After eighty years, she stated her work was "a treasure trove of hyperbole, adverbs and a fair amount of poetic license." Her journals are often the topic of obscure doctoral dissertations. She is seen here with her mother, Ollie.

Rupert Manning, seen here sporting a scowl a day before his demise, was a gas. Never one to avoid a quick jab or inappropriate joke, Rupert will be sorely missed by his landlady. Divorced and estranged from family for obvious reasons, Rupert intensely disliked bad poetry, puppies, and garish, uncouth women who dolled themselves up while refusing to accept dinner or a drink or whatever. His final words (reportedly) were a string of expletives.

29

Henrik Johansen, beloved husband of Meredith, and dearest father to Betsy, died peacefully in his sleep. Henrik first fell in love with Marilyn Monroe after she joked with him at a Venice beach hot dog stand. After months of personally delivering sunflowers to her office, Henrik married Ms. Monroe's secretary. Henrik loved to dance the cha cha. "It's like walking back and forth." He was also keen on Dirk Bogarde movies. "How can someone so good, be so bad?" No donations. Save the birds and the bees, plant sunflowers.

30

Randall Lovitz, physicist turned playwright, died as the result of an incident involving a grenade and a jigger of Hendricks. Mr. Lovitz's most recent play, *Naked Man Barking*, featuring 90 minutes of the same, was panned by the critics. An earlier production: *Knock, Knock... Who's there?... F__k.... F__k who?... F__k You...*garnered similar reviews. Always an iconoclast, the only holiday Mr. Lovitz celebrated was Super Bowl Sunday.

Herman Johnson floated into the state of Nirvana on Saturday. Forty years ago, Mr. Johnson left the family multi-million dollar business to pursue a life of enlightenment in Eureka, California. Mr. Johnson was well known in town as a herbalist, musician, and Reiki master. He often preached on street corners for change, of the spiritual and physical variety. In later years, he lamented he should have moved to Belize. "That place has wild energy."

Namke Lewis settled into the arms of the Lord on Saturday. The previous week Namke had made headline news after a nine-month court battle with New York State over KIS Psychic Services, her lucrative, subscription online company that only answered yes or no questions. The day before her passing, Ms. Lewis won her court case arguing that all KIS PS contracts, disclosures, and advertising clearly state her business "is for entertainment purposes only".

Lance Woodsman, on the eve of his 100th birthday, died peacefully at home. Mr. Woodsman, a retired biology teacher, fought tirelessly against the senseless killing of wildlife. He often attended town meetings with specific, entertaining flow charts showing how the ecosystem would change if certain animals became extinct. Segue topics included: how raccoons mate, where bears poop, why coyotes eat dead things.

Adelia Rosen passed over on Tuesday. She is survived by two daughters, Ade and Lia, and five grandchildren. At an early age, Adelia, known as Adelia Church, was to replace Shirley Temple after Shirley became a teenager. While photogenic with remarkable stage presence, Adelia often threw temper tantrums, refused to follow directions, and used foul language. Producer Darryl F. Zanuck was reported as saying "People would rather work with a rabid pitbull."

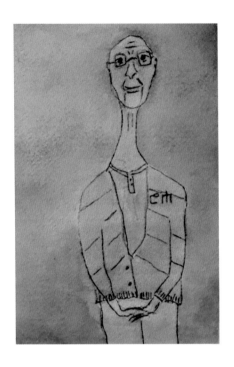

Creeley Messenger passed over in his 87th year. Mr. Messenger is survived by his wife, Pearl. A contemporary of Hermann Zapf, Creeley was an American typeface designer who worked extensively with Microsoft and Apple. His fonts became commonplace and renown throughout the world. Among the them, the Dinner Plate, a sans serif typeface based on cutlery. He second love to Pearl was making up pangrams. His more recent: *Foxy diva Jennifer Lopez wasn't baking my quiche.*

Sweet Pea (nee Agnes) Garrity passed over on Friday. She is survived by her loving husband, Roland, and brood of generations above and below. Sweet Pea, the youngest of 10 children, was coddled by her siblings until, at age 16, she rebelled by running off with Roland, a lanky boy with no sense who lived two doors down. Traveling in a beat-up Rambler, Mr. and Mrs. Garrity drove cross-country. It took them two years. Stops were frequent. "Sometimes it was that damn car. Other times we just dawdled looking up at the moon."

Charles Ambrose Longfellow died after a short illness. Mr. Longfellow, a lifelong resident of Martha's Vineyard, was key in many initiatives to have Martha's Vineyard secede from Massachusetts where the legislature had redistricted the island, stripping away representation. To mobilize the residents, Mr. Longfellow rallied the crowds with *Make It Ours.* He will be buried with the Martha's Vineyard Flag.

Dolly Warner reportedly died for the second time on Saturday. Mrs. Warner's first death was ten years ago after she was killed in a private airplane explosion. Her body was never recovered. Much to the shock of her widower, Jeffrey Warner, Dolly returned to town last year stating, having settled in Minnesota, she had been in a fugue state. After failed attempts to reconcile with Mr. Warner, Dolly became despondent and jumped into the lake at Lover's Bluff. To date no body has been found. Her death is being reported just in case.

Dear Friend,

Thanks for reading my book. If you'd like to pass along comments, inquires, objections, send an email to lindalavid@gmail.com with "Obits for Fun" in the subject line. Would love to hear from you!

Starry nights, Linda